by Brandon T. Snider

Grosset & Dunlap
An Imprint of Penguin Group (USA) LLC

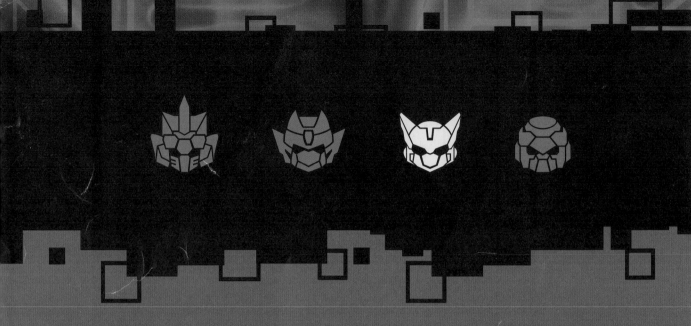

GROSSET & DUNLAP
Published by the Penguin Group
Penguin Group (USA) LLC, 375 Hudson Street, New York, New York 10014, USA

USA | Canada | UK | Ireland | Australia | New Zealand | India | South Africa | China

penguin.com
A Penguin Random House Company

TM Spin Master Ltd. All rights reserved. © 2014 Spin Master Ltd. / Shogaukuken-Shueisia Productions Co., Ltd. All rights reserved. Published by Grosset & Dunlap, a division of Penguin Young Readers Group, 345 Hudson Street, New York, New York 10014. GROSSET & DUNLAP is a trademark of Penguin Group (USA) LLC. Printed in the USA.

ISBN 978-0-448-48348-1   10 9 8 7 6 5 4 3 2 1

Long ago on the planet Quarton, a terrible war was fought over a resource known as Tenkai Energy. A group of noble warriors known as the Corekai fought to protect Tenkai Energy from falling into the hands of a warlord named Vilius and his evil followers known as the Corrupted. Only four valiant heroes could stop Vilius and save the planet . . .

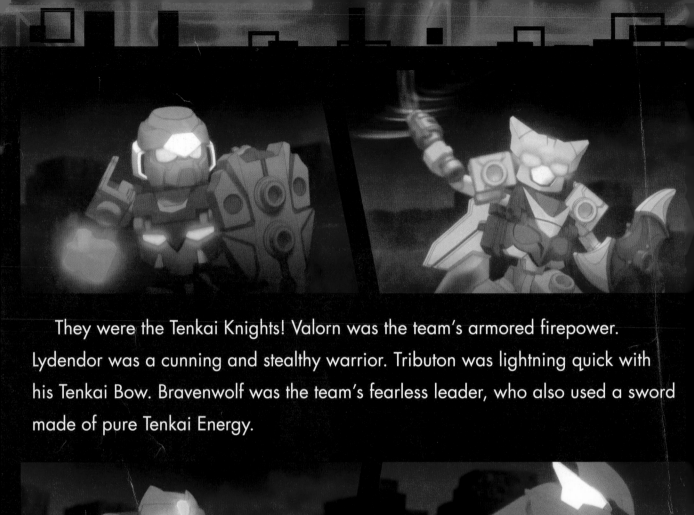

They were the Tenkai Knights! Valorn was the team's armored firepower. Lydendor was a cunning and stealthy warrior. Tributon was lightning quick with his Tenkai Bow. Bravenwolf was the team's fearless leader, who also used a sword made of pure Tenkai Energy.

The Tenkai Knights fought valiantly against Vilius and his mighty Tenkai Dragon. They were able to defeat the Dragon by combining their energy and scattering its pieces across the galaxy. After that, the Knights disappeared and were never seen again.

Now Vilius has returned, and the universe is in terrible danger. But where are the Tenkai Knights?

On Earth, a young boy named Guren Nash began his first day at a new school. Guren needed someone to help him find his way around. His teacher suggested that another student, Ceylan Jones, be his guide. Ceylan responded by letting out a loud burp. The boys laughed and knew they'd be fast friends.

Later, the boys went to the new Benham City Mall to hang out and have fun.

"Tenkai!" a voice whispered in Guren's ear as he spotted a strange figure heading into an antique shop. *Something weird is going on,* thought Guren. The boys followed the mysterious apparition into the shop.

The shop was filled with curious old items. The boys noticed two small Bricks under a glass case nearby. "Tenkai!" a voice whispered as the Bricks began to glow brightly.

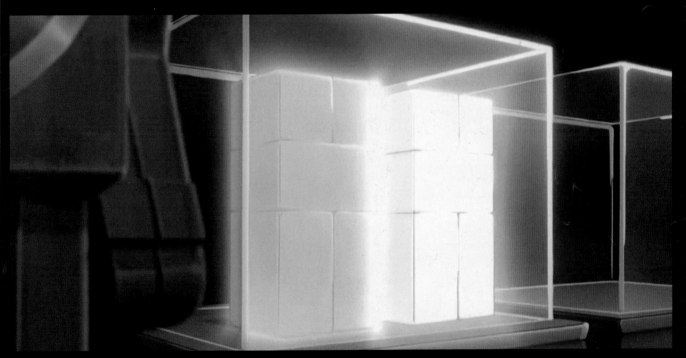

"Fascinating little Bricks, aren't they?" the shop owner asked. "Greetings, and welcome to the Shop of Wonders! My name is Mr. White."

"People with inquisitive minds and adventurous spirits are always welcome in my Shop of Wonders. There are priceless items here!" said Mr. White.

"Cool. Can I take a look at the white one?" Guren asked, pointing his finger at the Brick.

"Go right ahead!" said Mr. White. Guren grabbed the Brick, and it shapeshifted into a tiny robot figure. "You have a gift, young sir. Now each of you take a Brick and be on your way. We'll see one another again very soon, I assure you!"

"Tenkai!" a voice whispered, as the boys left the store.

Later that night, Guren wondered about his new toy. He shapeshifted the small robot back into a Brick and placed it on his pillow for safekeeping. Guren had many questions about where it came from, but first he needed a good night's rest to clear his mind.

Guren dreamed that he was the hero Bravenwolf, battling the evil warlord Vilius.

"The universe belongs to the strong. Watch me crush you with my Tenkai Dark Storm!" exclaimed Vilius.

Guren woke up and was very upset. "That was so scary and real. Was it all in my head?!" he wondered.

At school the next day, Guren told Ceylan all about his dream. "I was the robot from the shop, and I fought this other, evil robot!" he said.

"Wait a second! I had the same dream!" exclaimed Ceylan. "I bet it has something to do with those weird Bricks. Let's find Mr. White and get some answers."

Guren and Ceylan arrived at the Shop of Wonders, but Mr. White was nowhere to be found. After snooping around a little bit, the boys followed a secret door into the basement. Their Bricks began to glow, because something big was about to happen!

The boys uncovered another secret door that led them to a strange-looking device. As soon as they got near the device, it zapped them with a weird energy beam, causing them to vanish into thin air. But where did they go?

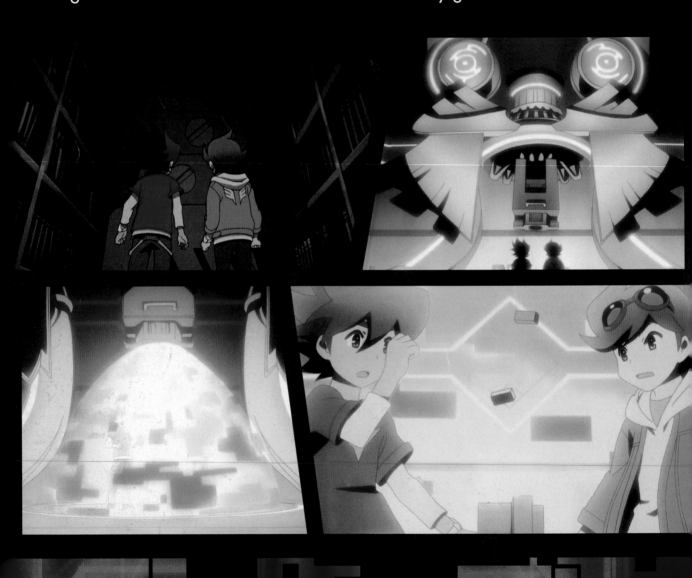

"Where am I?" Guren asked. Was he having another weird dream?

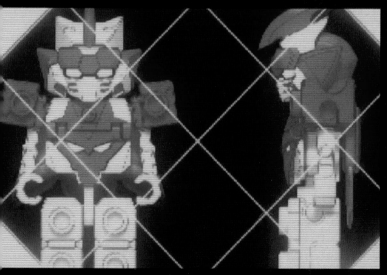

"You have been chosen to become Bravenwolf, a Tenkai Knight and hero of the Corekai," said a voice in Guren's head. "You are in the fortress of Vilius on the planet Quarton. I am your AI guidance system. This is not a dream."

"How did I end up inside this armor?!" Guren asked.

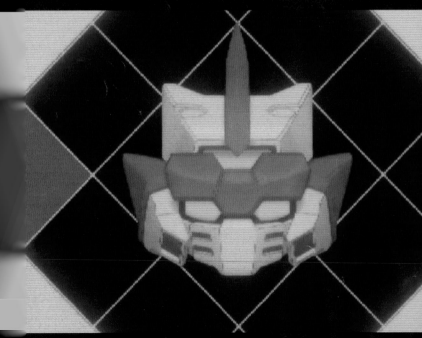

"You are not *inside* the armor, you *are* the armor," said the AI voice. "Your friend Ceylan has been chosen to become the Tenkai Knight known as Tributon, but he is trapped in his Brick form and needs to be activated immediately. Use your power to transform him!"

"I hope this works. Initiate Tenkai Energy Infusion!" said Bravenwolf. He changed his friend Ceylan into the powerful Tributon, and now they both were ready for action.

"This is totally awesome!" shouted Tributon.

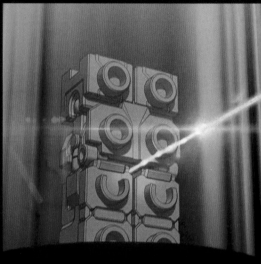

"We don't have much time," said Bravenwolf. "We have to get out of here!"

...ton and Bravenwolf activated their Tenkai Weapons and blasted out of th... ...but the Corrupted soldiers started attacking them from all directions. It loo... Tenkai Knights were in big trouble.

Suddenly, a blast of Tenkai Energy came down from the sky and destroyed the Corrupted army.

"You led the enemy right to us!" said Beag, the leader of the Corekai army. "The Tenkai Knights are back to lead us to victory! The heroes have returned!"

"Heroes, huh?" said Bravenwolf. "I guess we have some pretty big shoes to fill!"

Vilius and his evil
minions planned their
next attack from a
castle on the dark side
of Quarton.

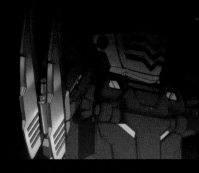

"I see the Tenkai Knights have returned," Vilius said. "Granox and Slyger: You are
both vicious warriors. Deal with Bravenwolf and Triburton once and for all. Do not
disappoint me."

"As Vilius commands!" shouted Granox and Slyger.

"Vilius and the Corrupted will return one day, but with the Tenkai Knights by our side, we will finally have enough strength to defeat them once and for all!" said Beag.

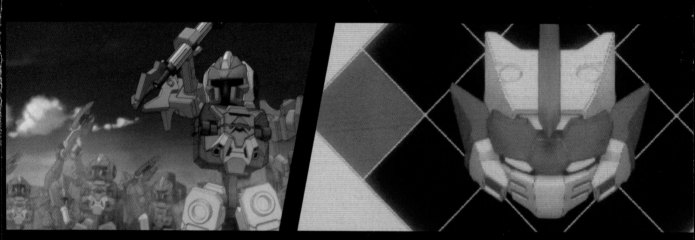

"Energy levels are low. Tenkai Portal engaged!" the AI voice said, transporting Bravenwolf and Tributon back to the Shop of Wonders.

"That was crazy. We were super roboheroes! Do you think anybody's ever going to believe us?" asked Ceylan.

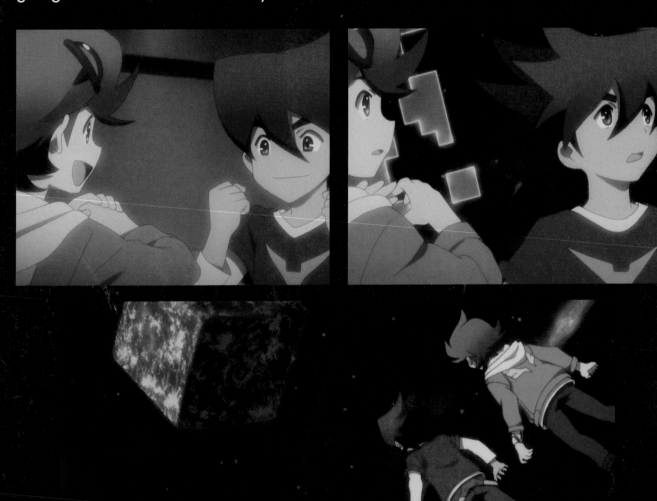

"I don't know. But I can't wait for what happens next!" said Guren.